AlloList

MW00942426

I'm Bernadette!

EMILY GRACE ORTEGA

illustrated by
Meg Ross Whalen

This is a work of fiction. Names, characters, places and incidents are either products of the author's imagination or, if real, are used fictitiously.

Text copyright © 2013 by Emily Grace Ortega.
Cover and interior illustrations copyright © 2013 by Meg Ross Whalen.
Published in the United States by Half Moon Bay Publishing, a division of Jacob Laskowski Company, LLC.

www.HalfMoonBayBooks.com/Im-Bernadette

All right reserved. No part of this book may be reproduced, transmitted, or stored in an information retrieval system in any form or by any means, graphic, electronic or mechanical, including photocopying, taping, and recording, without written permission from the publisher.

First written edition 2013.

www.HalfMoonBayBooks.com

to Mary Grace, who is always
looking for something good to read

-E.G.O.

for my parents, who have
always supported me

-M.R.W.

Contents

An Address from the Principal

CHAPTER ONE

St. Cletus is a new school, and I am a "founding student" there. We are called founding students because the founding is the beginning of something. We are the students beginning the school. Our principal, Sister Teresa Jerome, always calls us "founding students" when she addresses the whole school. She likes to address the whole school. She addresses us after almost every school

Mass, which means every Wednesday and every Friday. "Address" is the school word for "talk to." It is also the word for the number on your house, next to the front door. That's an interesting fact.

Today is the first day of October, and Halloween is coming up at the end of the month. I love Halloween for all the candy and the fun costumes. My friend Maggie loves it, too. I'm planning to dress up as Snow White this year. I think Maggie is going to be Tinkerbell.

After Mass this morning, Sr. Teresa Jerome was addressing us from the front of the church, at the microphone where the priest stands when he's doing his talk in the middle of Mass.

"Founding students!" she began. "I have a special announcement to make. In four weeks, we will have an All Saints' Day Celebration! This will be the Founding Celebration for our school, so we all want to work hard to make it especially celebratory and special. Who knows what 'celebratory' means?" She looked around to see if anyone knew.

A bunch of kids from second grade and one kindergartener raised their hands. I don't think the kid from kindergarten really knew what "celebratory" meant. Sometimes those little kids just raise their hands.

"Yes? Robert?" Sister said, and she pointed at Robert from the second grade.

"It means celebration-al," Robert said, very loudly so everyone could hear. I am in first grade, so I don't personally know Robert the Second Grader. But I do know that he always raises his hand when Sr. Teresa Jerome asks a question and that he always answers very loudly so everyone can hear and that he always is correct. These are the only things I know about Robert, which makes me wonder if there are other, more interesting things to know about Robert. Or does he just mainly think about answering questions loudly and correctly?

"Well. Yes," said Sister after Robert answered. "It means joyous and special and happy. Everything that makes a celebration. Which means that we will include games and treats for our Founding All Saints' Day Celebration. And the culmination—the best part—of this celebratory celebration will be the All Saints' Parade. Each of you will come to school in costume to look like a saint. Then, we will have a parade of saints all around the school grounds. I am sending a notice home today in your Friday envelopes so your parents will know all about it."

Friday envelopes are for notices and permission slips and finished projects and finished papers that are supposed to go to your parents. If you give the Friday envelope to your mom, you cannot be in trouble for things like forgetting to dress up on picture day. Your mom read about it in the Friday envelope, and she forgot, too.

We had to wait quietly in our pews while the kindergarten walked out of church. Then it was our turn. Maggie lined up single file behind me to walk back to our classroom. We do a lot of walking single file here at St. Cletus. Miss D, our teacher, leads the single file line. She likes it quiet in the halls, please.

Maggie waited until Miss D wasn't looking and whispered, "What do you think about an All Saints' Day Parade? I don't think that's as good as a Halloween party. I was going to be Tinkerbell. I even have fairy wings in my dress-up box. I even—"

"Quiet in the halls, please!" called Miss D quietly and cheerfully. Just about everything Miss D says, she says cheerfully. She's also the only person I know who can call things out quietly and the whole class can still hear what she said. I guess that is her special talent. Mama says I have special talents, too. But I have not found them out yet.

After that, Maggie had to stop whispering.

I faced front and single filed the rest of the way to the classroom without whispering. I'm working on not whispering. It is not easy when Maggie is always lining up behind me, but it was a little easier this time. I was thinking about how I agreed with Maggie. A Halloween party would be better than an All Saints' Day Parade.

Talent of Destruction

CHAPTER TWO

It's a good day when I do not have to wait too long for Mama after school. Today was not a good day. First we found out that, instead of a Halloween party, we were going to have an All Saints' Day celebration. Then I had to wait for Mama for a long, long time. When she did show up, I climbed into the minivan and buckled my seat belt.

"How was school today?" she asked me. She always asks this. "Where are your socks?" she asked.

I hadn't even answered the first question yet.

"Pretty good," I answered to the school question. I squiggled my feet out of my shoes and wiggled my toes. I do not like to keep my toes in their shoes. I looked at them. They looked happier already. "I think my socks are in my lunchbox. Because I took them off at recess. Because it was too hot for my toes."

That answered the socks question. Mama is always worried about my socks and shoes and where they are and is the dog going to eat them. I never worry about socks and shoes. But twice the dog has eaten my shoes. I am working on putting them away. I have so many things to think about that are much more interesting than socks and shoes. That makes it hard to remember.

It was quiet in the car for a moment. I

leaned forward, backwards and sideways in my seat. My littlest brother Matthew sat next to me, in his car seat. He sits in a baby car seat because he just turned one. My brother Victor, who is four, was at the other end of the row, next to the window. I leaned forward again. Victor and Matthew started making a lot of noise.

"What happened at school?" Mama asked me, pretty loudly so I could hear.

"Well. Sr. Teresa Jerome announced a founding concentration."

Mama scrunched up her face. "A founding concentration? What's that?"

"You know," I said. "We're all the founding students. And All Saints' Day is going to be the founding conflagration. That means the first one," I explained.

"The first what?" Mama asked. She looked up at the rearview mirror. "Victor, quiet down. Stop poking Matthew."

"The founding CONFABULATION!" I

said very loudly. "A PARTY with treats and games. Sheesh. Even Robert in Second Grade knew that."

"Give Spotted Ducky back to Matthew," Mama said to Victor in the backseat. "A party with . . . oh—I think you mean a celebration. An All Saints' Day celebration. That sounds very nice."

Then I was quiet and wiggled my toes. I rearranged the notices and papers in my Friday envelope. I turned and made a funny face at Victor. He tried to make the same face back at me, but he couldn't squiggle his nose up quite right, so he didn't look funny. He just looked odd.

Mama pulled the minivan into the driveway, and then she carried Matthew into the house. Victor and I followed her.

"Do you have any homework?" She asked me. Sometimes she forgets to ask this.

"Spelling," I groaned. "I hate spelling. I like letters. I like words. But I do not like spelling. It sneaks into my dreams at night and turns them into nightmares. It sneaks into my playtime and makes it sad time. I sneaks into my—"

"Oh," Mama interrupted me. "Today is Friday. I suppose you can do it tomorrow."

"I'll take the deal," I said. "There is one other thing, Mama. The celebration. I'm supposed to dress up as a saint. Everyone is supposed to dress up as a saint."

"How delightful!" said Mama. "Do you have any ideas of which saint you would like to be? Maybe you could look in your box of dress-ups to see if anything there would be a good costume."

Sometimes Mama has good idea. I wandered toward my room. I have my own room now. I used to share with Victor. But now Matthew shares a room with Victor. So I have my own room because I am the only girl. But I think maybe I would like a sister better than having my own room.

When I got to my room, Victor was there, with scissors in his hands. I looked around and saw small pieces of red cloth on the floor. He had pieces of my dress-ups everywhere. They were all cut to small pieces. He had ruined my sparkly red jacket. He had ruined the striped shepherd costume. He had ruined the veil of the bride costume. He was working on ruining the purple princess costume that has bells on it so you jingle when you walk.

"VICTOR!!! GET OUT OF MY ROOM!!!!" I pointed at the door. I screamed at him more, but he just held the scissors and looked at me. I grabbed the purple princess dress. I needed it to be in one piece, not ruined. I screamed and stomped and cried and screamed. Mama arrived at the door. She frowned at Victor with her mouth scrunched in a way that it only scrunches when she is very angry. She grabbed Victor by the collar on his green striped shirt and marched him to the door. I don't know where she marched him after that.

Like I said, Victor is four, so his special talent is destruction. He destroys blanket forts. He destroys block towers. He destroys Lincoln Log cities. He destroys dress-ups. I was so upset that he had destroyed my beautiful dress-ups that all I could do was cry.

Later, when my eyes were all cried out, Mama came back. I was just snuffling and trying to think of something that was not destroyed. Mama handed me a book. She pointed at the front and read the words as she pointed to them. I can read now that I am in first grade. But Mama still points to the words as she says them.

"Saints for Girls," she pointed and read. "I thought this might help you think of a saint costume. I am sorry Victor ruined so many of your dress-ups. He has been punished. Don't worry. We will still make sure you have a wonderful saint costume. Do you want me to look at the book with you?"

"No," I answered. "I don't want anyone."

Mama left. I looked at *Saints for Girls*. The first page had a pretty picture of Saint Monica. I looked at the picture more closely. St. Monica was crying. I did not want to be a crying saint. I was tired of crying. Maybe some of the other saints for girls would be more interesting.

Quick Decisions

CHAPTER THREE

On Monday morning, I slid into my desk in Room Two. Maggie was already sitting at her seat in the next row over. She said good morning and looked like she was about to say something interesting. Then Miss D rang the bell. That meant it was time to begin learning. So Maggie had to save up whatever interesting thing she was about to say. Miss

D is very nice, so Maggie and I try to behave and not talk when it is time for learning.

But learning time doesn't last forever, thankfully. When Miss D finally rang the bell that signaled the switch from learning time into morning recess time, we all lined up nicely and walked to the classroom door. We walked in our line through the hallway. We walked in our line to the playground door. Then, when we crossed through the playground door, we could finally forget all about that line. We burst out onto the playground. I ran to the slide. Maggie climbed the steps right behind me.

"Guess what!" she said as we climbed.

"What?" I asked. I was already at the top. The playground slide has twelve steps. That makes it pretty tall, but I am a fast climber.

"I know my saint costume!" Maggie shouted at me.

I slid down the slide. I did not say anything to her. I did not want to talk about saint costumes. I did not like that founding celebration idea, and I did not love this All Saints' Day problem.

I shuffled under the slide and kicked the wood chips. I tried to think of something different to play. I tried to think of something different to talk about. I kicked the wood chips again. I could see something bright pink by my shoe. A pink pencil with sparkly silver stars! I picked it up and brushed the wood chip dust off of it with the sleeve of my sweater. It was so sparkly and beautiful!

I poked the toe of my brown school shoes with the buckles around in the wood chips a little more. Nothing. I took a step out from under the slide and noticed something bright green by my toe. I kicked at it. A bright green pencil! I picked it up and polished it up on my sweater sleeve. Then I found a red pencil with golden squiggles on it. I poked around a little more but did not find any more pencils. Maggie came over. She was finished sliding now.

"Look what I found!" I said, "Three pencils! I am going to open a pencil store. Would you like to buy one?"

"I don't know," said Maggie. She was not too excited. "I don't have anything to buy them with. You didn't hear about my saint."

And then Maggie did not even wait for me to say *I don't care about your old saint costume. I don't care about the Founding Celebration.* She just kept talking.

". . . and the best thing about it is I can still wear my Tinkerbell wings! Because St. Gabriel is an angel. An archangel. And angels have wings! Isn't that great?"

Maggie did not wait for me to say if I

thought it was great. She kept talking.

". . . and I checked with Miss D about if archangels can count as saints. And she said they can."

"Hmmm," I said. "How about regular angels? Do they count as saints?" Maybe I could be a regular angel. That might be OK. They had pretty outfits. But the only angels with names I knew had boy names.

"I don't know about regular angels," Maggie said.

Well, so much for that idea.

"Isn't Gabriel a boy name?" I asked. Maybe Maggie couldn't make everything work out.

"My mom said that even though it is, angels are not really boys OR girls. So I can be the Archangel Gabriel. No problem. I'm going to be beautiful. With wings, and a long, lovely white dress and everything."

That was Maggie's talent. Making

everything work out just right. I think Maggie is the only kid I know who could manage to wear her fairy wings even though Halloween got changed to All Saints' Day. Forget about angels. I did not want to have the same costume as Maggie anyway.

"Well," I said. "How about buying a pencil?"

Maggie could not think of anything good to pay me for one of the pencils. So she became my salesperson. She can talk louder than I can, so that made her a good salesperson. She called out to our classmate Jeremiah, and pretty soon, he was under the slide, checking out the pencils. He offered me a popsicle stick and a broken rubber band for the green pencil.

"I'll take the deal!" I agreed and handed him the pencil.

"My costume is going to be St. John the

Apostle," he volunteered.

"Volunteered" means doing something when nobody makes you. Miss D is always asking for volunteers. Nobody made him tell me his costume. Nobody even asked for volunteers.

"What's St. John look like?" Maggie asked. She was interested.

"He wears a bathrobe. Because he was Jesus' friend. That was before they invented pants. I already have a brown bathrobe. And sandals. I hope it's not going to be too cold, though, because then my toes will freeze."

"Didn't St. John's toes freeze in the winter?" I asked.

"I guess that was before they invented winter," Jeremiah said.

Then our other classmates Victoria and Simon arrived at the pencil store, which made things pretty crowded under the slide, so Jeremiah had to go away. That was fine with me, because he just wanted to tell more about his bathrobe and sandals.

"We have two pencils left," I announced to my new customers, "pink and red."

"We'll give you a popsicle stick and a quarter for both of them," offered Victoria.

Victoria and Simon are twins. They mostly play together, and Victoria mostly does the talking. Simon mostly does everything else.

"Deal," I replied, and Simon handed me the popsicle stick and the quarter.

"Thanks," I said to Simon. To the rest of the playground I shouted, "The pencil store is closed! No more pencils."

Then we saw Miss D come out the door. That meant that she was about to ring the bell and change recess time back into learning time. So I ran to the stairs of the slide. I wanted to slide once more before learning time. Victoria and Simon followed me.

"Saints Benedict and Scholastica were twins," Victoria said, "like me and Simon, but a long, long time ago. So we're going to be them for All Saints'."

I slid down the slide. Miss D rang the bell. I ran to get in line before anyone else could tell me how great their All Saints' Day costume was going to be. My hand reached into my pocket and felt around. I had two popsicle sticks, a broken rubber band and a quarter, but I had no saint costume and no good ideas for one.

Dinnertime Disaster

CHAPTER FOUR

That night, I helped Mama set the table for dinner. She says that is my job now. Since I am a big girl in first grade, I have to help set the table for dinner every single night. Every night is a lot of nights. But tonight she made spaghetti and meatballs. Spaghetti and meatballs is one of my favorite dinners, so

I don't mind setting the table for that one. Mama said that when Victor is in first grade, he will also have a job. Then I won't be alone in having to do some work around here. I am looking forward to that.

I put all the plates around the table, one at each chair. Except for Matthew's chair. He still sits in the high chair, so he does not need a plate. He just uses his high chair tray. Then I put all of the napkins around. I folded a different shape for each person. This makes the napkins more interesting. Making things more interesting is the only way to have fun setting the table. Even then, it is not a lot of fun, but it is a little bit of fun. Then I put a fork on the left side of the plate and a knife on the right side of the plate. Except for Victor's plate. He needs to grow in responsibility before he is allowed to have a knife. I am not exactly sure what that means, but that is what Mama said when Daddy asked if Victor isn't old enough to cut his own meat yet. I think it means that not too long ago Victor threw his knife at Mama, and it cut her a little bit, and now he cannot have one. He's too young to understand he has to be careful with knives or, for that matter, scissors and dress-ups.

After the table was completely set, Mama started putting the food on the table.

"Bernadette," she said, "would you please call everyone to come sit down? Dinner is ready."

This sounds like an easy job. It is not. It is easy to call. But it is not easy to make people come. But sometimes it is interesting, so I started looking for people. Matthew was easy to find. He was sitting on the floor in the kitchen eating Cheerios off of the floor. He waved his empty blue plastic bowl at me when I came in.

"Hi, Matthew," I said. "Come in for dinner." He did not move, but that was OK. Mama would carry him in and buckle him into his chair.

I tried to find Victor. First I looked in his bedroom. No one. Then I looked in the toy room. Lots of Legos and wooden blocks. No Victor. Then I looked in the bathroom. No one. Then I looked in the backyard. Victor was there with Daddy. They were playing T-ball. Why did no one invite me to play T-ball? I just had to set the table and call everyone for dinner. I scrunched up my mouth into a grumpy face.

"Time for DINNER!" I called very loudly. Then I turned my back and marched toward the table. I think Daddy said something to me, but I was already too far away to hear. I sat down with a frown and crossed my arms.

"Oh, Bernadette," said Mama as she buckled Matthew into his high chair. "I forgot the Parmesan. It's on the counter. Could you get it, please? And the grater?"

She didn't notice how grumpy I was. I got the Parmesan and the grater. I put them on the table with a noisy thump. I sat down and folded my grumpy arms again. Mama still did not see how grumpy I was. Daddy and Victor tumbled noisily through the door.

"Victor's getting pretty good with the baseball bat!" Daddy announced to anyone who was interested. That did not include me. I was not interested.

"It's not baseball," I observed. "It's T-ball."

"But you use a baseball bat," Victor explained, as if I didn't know. "Because it's for getting used to playing baseball."

"Whatever," I said.

"Let us pray!" said Daddy.

We all prayed. I mumbled the words, but no one corrected me. Mama dished up all the food. I looked at my two meatballs with my grumpy eyes. I did not really want them now.

"Do you know the interesting thing about meatballs?" I began.

"Daddy said I can play T-ball with a team next spring!" Victor shouted, ignoring me.

"Well, that's rather far off still, Victor,"

Mama said, "But that sounds like a fun idea."

Matthew threw a handful of noodles at my head. One of them stuck to my face. Daddy looked up from his plate.

"You have a noodle on your cheek, Bernadette," he said, pointing to his own face.

"I KNOW!" I said, peeling it off, "I didn't do that! Didn't any—"

"But it's not that far away, is it, Mama?" Victor interrupted me again. "I mean, the spring? Because I want to play T-ball on a team. With team hats."

"Well, we'll have All Saints' Day and then Thanksgiving and then Christmas and then the rest of winter and Matthew's birthday, and then it will be spring," said Mama.

It was quiet for a moment. I looked around at everyone ignoring me and crunching their garlic bread into crumbs.

"Bernadette," Mama began, "Did you get a chance to look at the *Saints for Girls* book? Do you have any good ideas for your saint costume yet?"

That was it. Nobody had even noticed I was upset and now another question about my costume! I did not want to talk about that at all.

"Is that all that anyone cares about?" I shouted. "Nobody listens to me and nobody even looks at me until you want to know about my saint costume! I DON'T HAVE ONE! I looked at every page of that *Saints for Girls* book, and those are a big bunch of boring old saints that I don't want to be like. I want to be Snow White and I want to have Halloween, and I don't want everyone to ignore me and talk about T-ball and throw noodles at me and tell me I'm wrong, wrong, wrong! And no one is helping me!" Then the tears came into my eyes and I ran to my room and slammed the door.

A few minutes later, Daddy knocked softly on my door and came in. I was lying on my bed snuffling.

"Bernadette, you shouldn't slam the door. Can you try to work on that? And next time you're angry, you can run away, but please do not slam the door," he said.

I thought he was just going to tell me how wrong, wrong, wrong I was. But he did not.

Instead he said, "I understand that it's hard to be the big girl. I'm sorry we weren't listening to you. Sometimes our boys do make dinner crazy. Tell me about the saint problem."

So I told Daddy all about it. I told him about the founding celebration, and about Maggie's archangel costume, and the St. John the Apostle bathrobe costume, and the twin saints, and how everybody else had special talents and how I was just not especially good at anything.

"So all the saints with good outfits are already taken!" I grumped.

Daddy said, "Was that almost a smile?" and then he gave me a little tickle.

"Stop that!" I shouted, pushing his hand away. "You are not allowed to tickle me when I'm mad!"

But Daddy just tickled me more. I tried to tickle him, but Daddy is not ticklish. But he was laughing anyway. I was laughing, too. We both laughed and tickled until I could hardly breathe.

"Is there a saint of laughing?" I asked. "I'll be that one!"

Spelling Test Saints

CHAPTER FIVE

Mama had my list of spelling words in the car when we were driving to school the next morning. She quizzed me while we were driving. That could only mean one thing: spelling test. I don't know how Mama always knows when a spelling test is coming up, but she does. Maybe the Friday envelope says something about when spelling tests are going to be.

"Could," said Mama.

"C-O-O-D," I said.

"Noooo . . ." answered Mama, very slowly. "This is a rather difficult list. Could is C-O-U-L-D," she said. "Now you say it."

So I spelled "could." Then we spelled "would" and "foot" and "book." I could not remember them all, just book. For sure I could spell book. I could probably spell foot, but not for sure. I sighed a big sigh. It meant I was not looking forward to that spelling test, but I would have to do it anyway.

"Don't worry about it, Bernadette," Mama said. "We practiced the words together a lot. So even if you don't remember how to spell some of them, you tried your best. You'll get better at spelling as you get better at reading. It's easier to spell the words once you're used to seeing them written."

Mama pulled up to the drop-off zone at school. I unbuckled my seat belt. I picked up my backpack. I picked up my lunch box.

"Hop to it!" said Mama happily and clapped her hands. "You're not late now, but you will be if you don't get going!"

I opened the door and slid down from the tall seat onto the sidewalk. I wiggled my toes in their shoes. They were not happy crammed in there. My toes do not like to be trapped in school shoes that are walking on the cement sidewalk. They prefer dirt and rocks in the backyard. I slammed the car door. Slamming car doors is all right. You have to slam them just to make sure they are closed all the way. Bedroom doors are different.

Mama rolled the window down and blew me a kiss. She shouted, "C-O-U-L-D!"

I smiled and blew a kiss back. Then I skipped into the school.

After morning recess, Miss D passed out blank, lined paper and said, "Get a pencil and make sure it is sharp. Time for the spelling test!"

I chose a pencil from the can. It was already sharp. But Linus, who sits next to me, reached in front of me and got a pencil that needed to be sharpened, so he had to walk to the back of the room, where the pencil sharpener is, and we all had to wait for him.

Once everyone was ready, Miss D read each spelling word very slowly. Then she repeated them, giving us lots of time to write them on our paper. I wrote an answer for each word she read. It did not feel like I had very many words spelled correctly.

For every spelling word Miss D said, Linus quickly wrote something down. Then he smiled. Then he quietly danced his feet on the floor under the desk. By the tenth word, I was getting tired of all the quiet foot-dancing next to me. Linus has a special talent for spelling. He loves spelling. He would be happiest if we never did anything other than spelling at school. He does not like to draw. When we are supposed to draw, Linus just sits there and spins his pencil. Then he bites his eraser. Then he whispers to me, "What should I draw, Bernadette?" So I tell him what to draw. There are always plenty of good things to draw. I like drawing, and I can always think of something interesting to draw. But I do not have a special talent for drawing because no one can really tell what my pictures are about until I explain them.

We passed our spelling test papers in. Linus was so happy about his that he started giggling when he handed it to Miss D.

That made Miss D smile and say, "Did you do well on your spelling test, Linus?" she walked around and collected everyone's tests.

"I am pretty sure I spelled all of the words correctly," he answered. "I have a head for spelling," he continued. "That's what my Dad says. So I'm going to be St. Thomas Aquinas for All Saints' Day. My Dad says that St. Thomas Aquinas was a saint who liked to spell and pretty much always spelled everything correctly."

Miss D was back at the front of the classroom. She smiled again. "That's right," she said. "St. Thomas Aquinas was a very good student. Then he became a very good teacher. That's a great idea to dress as a saint with whom you share a talent. Is anyone else planning a costume of a saint who is a little bit like themselves?"

I felt droopy. How could I find a saint who had no special talents? Saints are only about special talents. Without a great special talent, a person would not be a saint. I could not think of a special talent I shared with a saint. I could not think of a good saint costume. I was starting to run out of time before All Saints' Day, and I was worried.

After Miss D finished talking about saints and talents and what different costumes some of the kids were going to wear, she announced it was lunchtime.

We don't have a separate room to eat lunch. We eat in the classroom. I opened my lunchbox and took out the food. Cheese sandwich. Cookie. Applesauce. I love applesauce. It is my favorite thing to have for lunch. I looked in my lunchbox again. It was empty. Mama had forgotten the spoon for the applesauce. October was starting to be a bad month.

A Saint for Bernadette

CHAPTER SIX

It was a no-homework day, so in my room after school, I found *Saints for Girls*. I was looking at the pages of the different saints, wondering if any of them would be a good costume. I was not worried that Mama would come in my room any minute and ask, "Did you finish your homework?" I like not worrying about that.

Instead of Mama, Victor came in. I did not

want to play with Victor just then. I wanted to look at my book.

"Bernadette," he started, "do you want to have a show?"

"No. You ruined my best costume for a show," I answered. I looked at my book some more.

"Bernadette," Victor started again, "Do you want to have an explore in the backyard?"

"No," I said.

Victor walked over to my dollhouse and started moving some things around.

"Bernadette," he said, "Do you want to make mud pies in the sandbox?"

"No!" I shouted. "I'm trying to read this book! I don't want to play with you!"

Victor just looked at me. He did not go away. Then Matthew walked in. He just learned to walk. It's fun to watch him, because he still looks like he will just tip over. Sometimes he does tip over. It does not hurt him, though. I watched his funny baby walk.

He walked right to the dollhouse and started chewing on the Mom-doll's leg.

"Matthew, NO!" I shouted.

He looked at me with big eyes. He kept chewing on the Mom-doll. I grabbed it away from him. He took the sister-doll and started chewing her arm. Victor laughed and grabbed the brother-doll and started chewing his head.

"No, no, NO!" I shouted at them both. I snatched the dolls away.

Matthew got the Dad-doll to chew. There were no dolls left. Victor took the fancy bed with the canopy and started chewing that.

"STOP!" I yelled. "STOP! STOP destroying my dollhouse!" I stomped my feet and yelled and tried to grab the dollhouse pieces away from those boys. Every time I got one away, they just started chewing up a different one. "STOP, STOP, STOP!" I shrieked. I cried and stomped and yelled at those boys.

Mama showed up at the door. "Oh dear,"

she sighed and shook her head at the boys. She picked up Matthew and carried him away. Victor got quiet and still. Mama came back and led Victor away by the hand. I followed to see their punishment. Mama zipped them into jackets and set them in the sandbox. Then she filled up the dinosaur watering can with water and gave it to them. They were happy building mud pies. I was still snuffling and crying.

"That's not fair!" I shouted at Mama. "That's not a punishment! They need a punishment!" I stomped my foot.

"Sometimes little boys don't really need a punishment. Sometimes they just need mud. What were you working on before they came and started pestering you?"

"Hmmph," I grumped and pointed to the saint book.

Mama sat me on her lap, and we looked at it together. It had a lot of pages. One saint for every page. Mama read the name of the saint, and we looked at the pictures together.

St. Elizabeth of Hungary

St. Hedwig

St. Monica

St. Maria Goretti

St. Gertrude

St. Margaret Mary

St. Therese

St. Anne

Some of them looked pretty in their pictures. Some of them looked boring. Some of them had funny names. Some of them were from super long ago and wore funny clothes. Some of them were from not too long ago and wore regular-looking clothes. Lots of them were nuns. St. Hedwig was a queen. St. Monica was crying. St. Margaret Mary was holding a big medal. St. Anne was standing with a little girl. The girl was her daughter, who grew up to be the mother of Jesus. None of the ones who seemed interesting had pretty names. And none of the ones with pretty names had

good costumes. And none of the ones with good costumes were interesting. This made it impossible to find the one I should be for All Saints' Day. I really did not want to be a boring, old, ugly-named saint.

We turned some more pages.

St. Agnes

St. Teresa of Avila

Sts. Felicity and Perpetua

St. Catherine of Siena

St. Bernadette

"St. Bernadette?" I asked Mama.

I looked at the picture. In it, she looked nice and like she was not yet grown up. She wore a long brown skirt with a bright red apron tied around it. She had a pretty white blouse with tiny flowers dotted all over it like polka dots. It had buttons up the front and puffy sleeves. She had a scarf covering up most of her head and tied under her hair. It was bright blue with fringes on the edges, and it made the point of a triangle on the back of her head. She had big brown eyes that gazed up at a lovely picture of Mama Mary standing in a cave. A little lamb with a curly white coat stood behind Bernadette.

"Yes. St. Bernadette," answered Mama. "When she was a girl, she saw Mother Mary in a cave called the grotto."

Mama read me the page about St. Bernadette. I was beginning to like her. She sounded nice. She looked nice. She had lived in a town called Lourdes in France and had seen Mama Mary. She dug up a little stream in the grotto where she saw Mary. A boy who was blind put the water from the stream on his eyes, and he could see again. Many, many sick people put the water from the stream on themselves and got well.

"I went to Lourdes once," said Mama. "That was before I even knew Daddy. It is a lovely place. The stream is still there, and it is so quiet and peaceful. I have a prayer card from there. I'll go look for it."

Mama came back a few minutes later and handed me the prayer card. It had a picture of St. Bernadette on one side. Her costume was almost the same as the one in the book. She was just wearing different colors on the card. On the other side it read, "I love everything that is little."

I read it. It did not make sense to me.

"That means she found the peace of God and Mama Mary in things that were not important to most people. In the quiet at her cave—the grotto. In helping make dinner. In gathering firewood for her family. She never became an important person while she was alive. That made her happy."

"Do you mean she had no special talent?" I asked. I could not believe it. She saw Mama Mary! How could she have no special talent?

"Well . . ." Mama was thinking about this question. "I think no one could see her special talent. But Mama Mary could see the goodness deep in her heart. That is why

Mama Mary came to talk to St. Bernadette. Because of that goodness deep inside her that other people did not see."

"I will be St. Bernadette for All Saints' Day!" I said with a giant smile.

The Bernadette Costume

CHAPTER SEVEN

"I think St. Bernadette is a wonderful choice!" said Mama. She smiled at me. "I have to get dinner ready," she continued. "Why don't you think about your costume and maybe draw some pictures of how it should look. Then we can start working on it tomorrow. For St. Bernadette, we might have everything you need without sewing anything."

"OK," I said. I was still very happy about the idea for the costume. It would be fine to just keep the idea in my head until tomorrow. While the idea was just in my head, I could make my Bernadette costume perfectly perfect. In the meantime, I put the prayer card on my bookshelf, in the most special place I could think of: between *Little House on the Prairie* and *Heidi*.

The next day was Friday. I could hardly wait for learning and playing at school to be over so that I could start putting my St. Bernadette costume together. All day, I was thinking of what I might be able to use for it. I was thinking and thinking. Then I had the idea that I could wear the ruffled skirt that I got for my birthday. I was trying to remember if the St. Bernadette in the picture had a longer skirt or a shorter one. The skirt I got for my birthday is below my knees but not quite to my ankles. It is the longest skirt I have, but maybe St. Bernadette in the picture had a longer one. I could not remember for sure. Just as I was not remembering for sure, Linus kicked me gently under the desk.

"Hey!" I whisper-shouted at him.

He opened his eyes really widely at me and then nodded his head in the direction of Miss D at the front of the classroom.

Then I heard Miss D say, "Bernadette?" I could tell it was already the second time she had said my name. I looked at the blackboard. I could not tell what the question was.

"I'm sorry, Miss D. I wasn't paying attention," I admitted. I was so embarrassed. But Miss D says it is best to just say the truth when you are not sure what to do. Miss D gave me a small frown. She was disappointed in me for not paying attention. I felt even more embarrassed then because I hate to disappoint Miss D. She repeated the question for me. It was math, and it was not difficult, so I could answer it correctly. I was relieved I did not have to disappoint Miss D with a sad truth again, and I made sure to pay better attention for the rest of the day. When school finally ended that afternoon, Mama was already in the parent pick-up area when I came outside. That made a nice ending to the school day.

I hopped into the minivan. I tossed my Friday envelope on the floor by my feet and reached way out to pull the door shut. I buckled my seatbelt.

"Mama!" I looked at her with big eyes. "I've been thinking about my St. Bernadette costume all day! Have you been thinking about it? Because I have a few ideas but also a few questions, and I'm not sure exactly what clothes St. Bernadette would have worn. Because how long ago was she living? And she did not live in this country, did she? Was her country called Frank? Did they wear a different kind of clothes in Frank?

I mean, not Frank. France. Because I was thinking that maybe I don't have any clothes that are like France clothes because that's a different country and also from a long time ago. But maybe the skirt that I got for my birthday would be just right? The one that is dark, dark red with the little pink birds on it. Because I think it is just about the same shape as the skirt St. Bernadette is wearing in the picture. I am not sure if it is quite as long as St. Bernadette's, though. What do you think?"

"Whoosh!" Mama said. "Slow down a bit, Bernadette! I think I did not quite follow all of your thoughts. I'm glad you're so excited about your costume. I do think that the dark, dark red skirt will be just right. That's a great idea. Let's see what else we can find for your costume when we get home."

As soon as I got home, I put on the skirt. I looked a lot like St. Bernadette already. I still had my school shirt on, which is navy blue with a collar and three buttons at the top. It did not look like a St. Bernadette shirt, so I opened my drawer with shirts in it. I took out the lavender one with three big flowers on it and spread it out on my bed. Then I looked in my closet to see if I had any blouses that would look more like a St. Bernadette one. I took out a white blouse with short, puffy sleeves and spread it next to the lavender shirt. Then I took out a pale yellow blouse with long sleeves that were not puffy and spread it next to the other two. It was hard to tell for sure which would be the best.

I took the prayer card of St. Bernadette off of my bookshelf and looked at it. Then I looked at the shirts again. I put on the white blouse. It looked like a pretty good one for a St. Bernadette. I guess France clothes from a long time ago are not really so different than my clothes. I looked at the picture again. I was getting close, but St. Bernadette wore some extra things on top of her regular

clothes. She had an apron over her skirt, a kind of vest over her blouse and a kerchief on top of her head. I took the picture to the kitchen and showed Mama St. Bernadette's outfit.

Mama smooshed her lips together and looked up at the corner of the ceiling like she does when she's really thinking. "I know!" she said.

She turned and left the kitchen, and Matthew and I followed her into her closet, where she pulled out a box with a lot of ribbons. Underneath all the ribbons, she found a red bandana like a cowboy would wear, a thin blue kerchief that was so delicate you could see through it and a shiny green kerchief with big red roses all over it.

"Would one of these be good for St. Bernadette?" Mama asked.

I thought about it. They all looked beautiful. I took the shiny green kerchief. It felt so smooth between my fingers, almost like something a princess would wear.

"This is the perfect kerchief!" I said to Mama. My lips were smiling and so were my eyes. "Do you have the perfect apron in here, too?" I asked, looking around the closet. Mama's closet was big and has many wonderful things in it. You can walk right into it, and then you're surrounded by clothes and shoes and some books and small boxes on shelves. Up high, there are big boxes and suitcases. There could be just about anything in that closet.

"No, I don't think I have the perfect apron here," Mama replied. "Let's go back to the kitchen. It might be there." She scooped up Matthew, and we all headed back to the kitchen.

I looked around skeptically. Mama folded the shiny green square kerchief into a triangle, put it around my head and tied it at the back of my neck, underneath my hair. It felt beautiful. She stepped back and looked at me. Then she nodded and bent over to open a drawer. She took out a cream colored tablecloth. She folded it into a big triangle and tied it around my waist.

"It IS the perfect apron!" I exclaimed. "I wasn't too sure you would find it in the kitchen!"

Mama laughed. "You never know!" she said.

I looked down at my apron. It would have been a little more perfect with fringe around the edges. But the corner had a lovely arrangement of yellow squashes and orange pumpkins with some green leaves curling around them. That made the apron look very special. I just needed a vest.

"I can't think of anything to be a vest right now," Mama said. "Let's think about that one over the weekend."

I wore my St. Bernadette costume the rest of the day, right until it was time to put pajamas on. I thought maybe Mama Mary would visit me in my dreams because I looked so much like her friend St. Bernadette. But she did not come. That's OK. She was probably busy.

A Vest and a Lamb

CHAPTER EIGHT

Mama Mary didn't visit my dreams that night, but St. Bernadette did. I dreamed that I was collecting firewood in the grotto— the little cave by the river where the real St. Bernadette met Mary in France. I picked up a nice big stick, and when I looked up, another girl was looking at me.

"Hello," she said, smiling. She had a

sweet smile that was not just in her lips. Her lips smiled, but so did her whole face, especially her eyes. Her eyes smiled full of quiet happiness.

"Hello," I said. I was wearing my Bernadette costume in my dream. Then I noticed that over her hair, she had a shiny, silky green kerchief with red roses on it. It looked exactly like mine!

"That's a lovely kerchief," I said to her.

"Thank you," she replied.

I noticed her apron. The corner was decorated with a yellow squash surrounded by orange leaves. Just like mine!

"That's a beautiful apron," I told her.

"Thank you," she replied again.

I noticed her vest. It looked soft and blue, just like in the picture. I looked down at my own blouse. I was not wearing a vest over it.

"That's a nice vest," I said.

"Thank you," she replied a third time. "My mother sewed it for me."

"Are you St. Bernadette?" I asked the girl. She looked surprised.

"My name is Bernadette," she answered, "But I am not a saint! I'm just a girl—like you! I'm gathering up firewood for my family. My sister is over there—" she pointed to another, bigger girl—"with our sheep. I need to go back and help her. Good-bye!"

She ran off and was gone.

I woke up, and it was the morning. I thought about my dream. I think the girl in my dream was St. Bernadette. I think I met St. Bernadette before she was a saint, before she saw Mama Mary. She was just a regular little girl—like me!

I went out to the kitchen to see who was awake and find some breakfast. It was Saturday. No one else was in the kitchen yet. Then I saw something on the back of my chair. The chair was in its regular spot, pushed in under the kitchen table. But hanging on the back of the chair was something that looked soft and dark blue. I walked over to the chair and looked closer. It was a vest! I picked it up off of the chair. It was the size for me! Mama found me a vest for my Bernadette costume! I slipped both of my arms through the armholes and tried it on over my flowery lavender nightgown. It fit perfectly! How did Mama do it? I wanted to run and give her a big hug and make her tell me how she got a soft, blue vest—just like the one in my dream!— in the middle of the night. But I did not run right to her, because she was still in bed. I figured she would be happier about getting a hug after she woke up.

I looked around. No one else was awake yet. So, I got a graham cracker out of the cupboard. Mama keeps them in the cupboard the kids can reach so we can help ourselves on mornings she doesn't have to get up early. Then I watched cartoons and ate my cracker. After one episode of "Cathy the Camel," Victor came in. Then we changed channels and found "Parade of Trains." Halfway through, we heard Matthew waking up. I went into his bedroom and pulled him out of his crib so he could watch the train show with us. Matthew likes trains a lot, even though he always breaks the tracks when we are building wooden trains.

After the trains had all delivered their cargo and were back at the depot, Mama came in.

"Mama!" I shouted, "Do you love my vest? I love it! It looks exactly like St. Bernadette's. I know because I had a dream of her, and she had a vest exactly the blueness and exactly the softness of this one! Where did it come from? Did St.

70

Bernadette come in the night and leave it like St. Nicholas brings gifts in the night?"

Mama smiled really big and yawned. Then she looked around and yawned again. Then she remembered that my words included a question.

"I sewed it for you," she answered. "I remembered that I had some blue felt left from making the felt flowers for your birthday party last year. I checked, and I had just enough. Felt is wonderful because I didn't even have to sew all the way around the edges, so I could do it in one night. See, I just had to do four seams."

Then Mama traced her finger up my side, across my shoulder, across my other shoulder and down my other side. Those were the four seams she had sewn to make my St. Bernadette vest. A seam is the line the thread makes where it sews through the cloth. I know that because Mama is

teaching me to sew.

"Is your costume just right now?" Mama asked me. "I can't think of anything else that it needs."

I scrunched my mouth up so that I could think about anything else my costume might need.

"I'm not sure," I answered. "I better double check. I'll let you know."

I went to my room and took the prayer card of St. Bernadette out from its special place on my bookshelf. I looked at the St. Bernadette in the picture. She had a kerchief, a skirt, a blouse, an apron, a vest and short black boots. I was planning to wear my brown school shoes with buckles. I thought those would be pretty good. So, I had almost everything that St. Bernadette did. The Bernadette in the picture had one other thing. She was petting the little lamb that stood next to her. That's because she took care of her family's sheep. Where could I get a lamb? That was the last thing I needed to make a very good costume a perfect costume.

Then I had the perfect idea about where to find a lamb. I went to the boys' room. I went over to Victor's bed and smoothed out his frog quilt. Nothing. I opened up his frog quilt and smoothed out the brown blanket under it. Nothing. I pulled the frog quilt and the brown blanket and the police cars sheet off of his bed. Aha! Just what I was looking for! Squished between the wall and the bed was Agnes, Victor's stuffed lamb. I pulled out Agnes and smoothed her down. She would be the perfect lamb for St. Bernadette.

Then Victor came in. "Hey!" he shouted, "That's my Agnes! You give me my Agnes back. I need it." Victor grabbed for Agnes the Lamb.

"Stop it!" I shouted back at him. "I was going to ask you. You didn't even give me a chance to ask if I could borrow it!"

Victor tugged at Agnes' head, but I did not let go of her feet. He tugged and shouted. I tugged and shouted. He shouted louder. I let go of the lamb, and Victor fell down with a loud thump, tumbled backwards and hit his head on the closet door. Victor started to wail and cry.

Daddy came in. He was wearing his dark blue bathrobe and rubbing his eyes and looking a little bit grumpy because he just woke up to a bunch of shouting kids.

"I'm sorry we woke you up, Daddy," I offered sheepishly.

Victor kept wailing. "She took my lamb!" he hollered. "She took my Agnes, and she can't do that because it's mine!"

Daddy looked at me. Then he looked at my hands. Then he looked at the floor where Agnes had tumbled between Victor and me.

"I was planning to ask him if I could borrow it," I said. "But he just started shouting and tugging, and I couldn't even ask, so then we were both—"

"QUIET!" Daddy shouted. When Daddy shouts, it can be louder than Victor and Matthew and me all put together. We were quiet. We were looking at Daddy.

"Bernadette," he began, "Why are you taking Victor's lamb? You know that's his special lamb that he always sleeps with."

"I DO know that," I agreed. "Everyone knows that. But I was not taking it. I was just trying to borrow it. Because I'm trying to be St. Bernadette, and she was a little shepherdess who took care of little lambs like Agnes. But he started shouting and grabbing before I could even ask."

"I see," said Daddy, rubbing his eyes. "Victor, may Bernadette borrow Agnes for her All Saints' Day costume?"

"No," pouted Victor. His bottom lip stuck out so far that a bird could have landed on it if there were any birds in our house.

"Can she take out a loan on it?" Daddy asked.

"What's a loan on it?" Victor asked. He was suspicious of this.

"A loan means that you let her use the lamb when she needs to. When she's finished with it, she gives it back to you along with something else. A little bit like a payment. Bernadette, will there be candy at your All Saints' Day celebration?"

"I think so," I answered. Now I was suspicious.

"Victor, how about you let Bernadette use the lamb for her All Saints' Day celebration.

After the celebration, she gives Agnes back to you along with two pieces of candy. You get to keep the lamb and the candy."

Victor was still a little suspicious. "Do I miss any nights of sleeping snuggled up with Agnes?"

"No, Bernadette just takes her to school on All Saints' Day," Daddy answered.

"I'll take the deal!" Victor exclaimed.

"Good," sighed Daddy. "I'll take some coffee!" He shuffled off toward the kitchen.

The Founding Celebration

CHAPTER NINE

Finally and at long last! It was All Saints' Day. I woke up before Mama even came into my room to wake me up. I put on my white blouse and my long, dark red skirt with the tiny pink birds on it. I put on my soft blue vest. I went to the kitchen to find Mama. She brushed my hair and divided it straight down the middle. She put one side in a ponytail.

Then she braided the other side. Then she went back and braided the first side. Two even braids made little trails down to my shoulders. Then Mama folded the shiny green kerchief with red roses into a triangle, put it over my head and tied two of the points under my braids. The third point pointed down the middle of my back. Then she tied on my tablecloth apron so you could see the squash and pumpkin and leaves in the front. I ran to the bathroom to have a look at my St. Bernadette self. I looked just like the St. Bernadette in the prayer card. I had to finish doing all of the regular things I do to get ready for school—eat breakfast, brush my teeth, find my other shoe, get my backpack. At last I got in the car with Mama. But I wasn't completely ready yet. I had forgotten Agnes! I got back out of the car, found Agnes and got back into the car with her.

The first thing at school for All Saints' Day was Mass. So we met our classes in church without going to our classrooms first. We are always supposed to be quiet in the church, but that was so hard! There were so many wonderful costumes to look at! All of the teachers were shushing all of the kids. All of the kids were looking and pointing at all the other kids' costumes. Sr. Teresa Jerome was in the back of church looking positively grim. I have heard Mama say "positively grim" about Grandpa when he did not get a morning coffee. I don't know if Sr. Teresa Jerome had a morning coffee, but she was not happy about noisy and excited kids being in the church. It did not matter if the kids were dressed like saints or not.

Sister walked through the church, bent down to one knee when she got to the front and climbed the three steps to the place where the microphone is. Everyone who was quiet stayed quiet. Everyone who was pointing faced front. Everyone who was whispering stopped. A few of the big kids knelt down on their kneelers like they were praying. I suspect that they were not praying.

"Founding students!" Sr. Teresa Jerome called. "Founding students, today is a great solemnity of Mother Church as we celebrate all the saints in heaven. It is also a great day for St. Cletus Academy as we commence our founding celebration. However, each of you knows the behavior that is expected of a St. Cletus student in church, waiting for Holy Mass to begin. Nothing less than that is expected of you now. You will have the opportunity to explain and share your costumes and saint stories with your classmates. This opportunity will come to you AFTER Mass, OUTSIDE the church. If the appropriate behavior does not commence immediately, I will be forced to cancel the All Saints' Day Parade.

"Additionally—which means also—the gentlemen should remove their headgear in the church." She looked around the church as if she would like to ask who knew what "headgear" meant. Instead, she continued, "Hats are never appropriate for gentlemen indoors, especially in church. This includes helmets, chain mail, scarves and anything else on the head."

Then she spotted Robert from second grade. He was sitting just across the main aisle from me, so I could see his face. He appeared to be someone from Jesus' time. He was wearing a halo. It looked like he didn't know if his halo counted as headgear or not.

Then Sister continued, "Halos are acceptable for both gentlemen and ladies—only on All Saints' Day. Ladies may wear head coverings in church, as a lady covering her hair is a sign of respect. So, ladies may continue to wear their hats, bonnets, kerchiefs, veils and other head accessories." She paused and glanced around. "If we have a St. Joan of Arc—I don't see one, but she may be here—who is wearing a helmet,

I believe that St. Joan would opt to remove her helmet, since a helmet is generally more suited to men on the battlefield than women seeking to be respectful of God in church. I would recommend anyone in a St. Joan of Arc costume do the same."

I looked down at my feet. I had not really been whispering to anyone. Maybe I just had not had time to whisper since I had only been in my spot with Miss D's class for a moment before Sr. addressed us. I peeked at Maggie, who was in the pew right next to me. She put down the kneeler and closed her eyes and bowed her head like she was the saintliest saint that ever prayed. I wondered what she was praying. Her angel wings sure looked nice and fluttery and sparkly. I knelt down, too, and started the "Good morning, dear Jesus" prayer in my head. I had already prayed it out loud in the car with Mama, but I could not really think of another good prayer for the morning. I did not have to, because then the little bell at the back of church rang, and we all stood up because that meant that Father Brookstone was coming in and Mass was beginning.

We sang:

For all the saints,
who from their labors rest
May you, oh Jesus, be forever blest.
And in our hearts, take u-u-u-p Thy rest
A-a-lle-e-lu-ia, A-a-a-llelu-u-ia!

We had been practicing it for a while with Miss Faith, the music teacher. So by now, we could remember most of the words. We sang all of the verses. My favorite part is the Allelulias, because you get to stretch them out as you sing, then make your voice go up and down. It's a fun way of singing.

After Mass, the parade began directly. We walked out of the church and started a big loop around the school.

As soon as we were out of church, Maggie

was next to me asking, "Who ARE you? I can't even tell!"

"I'm Bernadette!" I answered. "I'm SAINT Bernadette!" I twirled around to let my skirt and my tablecloth apron swirl out. I love twirling when I'm wearing a nice skirt.

"Hey! That's pretty great!" said Maggie. "I like the squashes on your apron."

"Thanks," I replied. "I love your wings. They're so sparkly!"

Then our classmate Genevieve showed up next to us.

"Who are you?" Maggie asked her. "Are you Mother Mary?"

"No, I'm not," answered Genevieve.

"You look like her," Maggie observed a little suspiciously. "Especially with that veil."

"But look!" answered Gen, and she took off her veil. It had a kind of picture of Jesus on it. "I'm St. Veronica!" she exclaimed. "Jesus put a picture of Himself on her veil when she wiped His face just before He was crucified.

My dad drew this one on an old napkin for me. Didn't he do a great job? It looks so good!"

Genevieve was right. Her dad really had done a great job drawing Jesus' face on her veil.

Then Miss D came over to help our class line up for the parade. It was a double file line, so we needed a little help. We're used to walking single file, but double file was new to us. Miss D said the parade would stretch out too far if we went single file, but we could switch places with the person next to us if our parents ended up on the other side. She looked at all of us after we were finally lined up.

She was smiling and admiring. She recognized most of the costumes since so many kids had been telling everybody whom they were dressing as. Then she looked at me.

"Bernadette, tell me about your costume, please," she said nicely.

"I'm Bernadette!" I exclaimed, twirling so my skirt would flare out. "I'm SAINT Bernadette! And this is my lamb," I added, holding up Agnes.

The Starry Crown

CHAPTER TEN

The parade began. We all marched and smiled and waved. Most of the moms, some of the dads, and lots of little brothers and sisters were lined up to wave at us and smile as we paraded around the whole outside of the church and then in front of the school. Mama was there with Victor and Matthew.

They were both wearing black clothes, with a stripe of white tape at their necks, so they would look like they had priest shirts on. They also had jungle hats on their heads. Well, Victor had a jungle hat on his head. Matthew was holding a jungle hat and chewing on the edge of it.

"What saints are you guys?" I shouted at Victor as my class was parading past them.

"We are Mission Cherries!" he called happily. "You can tell by our pit helmets!" he waved his hat.

I did not know what a Mission Cherry was, but whatever it was, it did not sound like a great saint costume to me. But I smiled and shouted, "You look great!" I was so happy with my own Saint Bernadette costume that it was OK with me if Victor and Matthew wanted to be Mission Cherries.

"They are missionaries!" called Mama. "Missionaries to the hot jungles. Missionary saints whose names have been lost to history. The hats are called pith helmets. They are good for keeping off the sun and the rain of the jungle."

Then I recognized the hats. Mama had bought them at the zoo one time when Grandma and Grandpa came to town. The one Matthew was wearing was really mine. That was OK, too. After all, I had a borrowed lamb. He could use a borrowed hat—even if he forgot to ask. I waved some more at Mama and Victor and Matthew. Daddy had come to Mass—I saw him—but then he had to go straight to work, so he was not with them.

Miss D started our class in singing:

Oh when the Saints!
Go marching in!
Oh when the Saints go marching IN!
Oh, Lord, I want
To be in that number!
Oh, when the Saints go marching IN!

We had been practicing this song, too.

It was a great marching song. Maggie and I could sing it louder than anybody. That is a fun thing about singing in a parade. The singing can be very loud. Miss D kept adding more verses, and we kept singing all the way back to our classroom. It was a wonderful founding celebration!

We sat down at our desks. After all the treats were shared around and we all had a cup of hot cinnamon cider, I made sure to get two pieces of candy to give to Victor for letting me borrow Agnes.

Then, Miss D clapped her hands and said, "Class! Our founding celebration is not quite complete! Saints in heaven wear a crown of victory. So, we too will wear crowns."

She took out a beautiful, gold crown and put it on her head. Tiny stars were connected to it and stuck out all around it. It looked something like tinsel for a Christmas tree, but even more beautiful.

Miss D continued, "Jeremiah's mom

and Linus' mom—Mrs. Cross and Mrs. Gallagher— are helping us make the crowns. Please be patient and wait for your turn."

After I had my crown made, I put it on my head, right on top of my kerchief. I peeked at myself in the tiny mirror at the back of the room, next to the water fountain. I looked like a perfect Saint Bernadette with my perfect costume, my little lamb and a starry crown. What a perfectly perfect founding celebration. I could not even think of how being a real saint in the real heaven with a crown of real stars could be more perfect.

+jmj+

meet the author

Emily Ortega earned a Bachelor of Science in Chemistry from Case Western Reserve University. After working for two years as a campus missionary with FOCUS, the Fellowship of Catholic University Students, Emily earned her Masters degree in Humanities from Stanford University. *I'm Bernadette* is her first published book. She currently resides in Santa Fe, New Mexico, with her husband and their six children.

meet the illustrator

Meg Whalen was born in Michigan, but grew up in Florida near the ocean. She has always enjoyed drawing and had a comic strip when she was a girl, but it wasn't until much later that she decided to pursue a career in children's books. After converting to Catholicism, Meg moved to Colorado to study theology at the Augustine Institute and to train in illustration at Rocky Mountain College of Art & Design. She resides in Denver with her husband, Danny.

Coming in 2014:

Christmas
with Bernadette!

EMILY GRACE ORTEGA

illustrated by
Meg Ross Whalen

Half Moon Bay
PUBLISHING

A Sneak Peak at the first chapter of
Christmas with Bernadette!

Ch. 1: It's Beginning to Look a Lot Like Advent

I hopped into the minivan after school. It had been a great day, and Mama's car was already there waiting for me. That made it a really great day. "Mama!" I exclaimed as I climbed up into the car, "Advent! Did you know that Advent is starting up on Sunday? That means we're coming right up toward Christmas!"

"Christmas?" Victor asked from the backseat where he was buckled, "For real, Bernadette? Christmas?" Victor is four. He barely remembers last time we had Christmas. A few times in the summer we snuck into the storage closet together and got out our Christmas stockings. We just wanted to look at them. They're so beautiful. Mine is dark, dark red with sparkly snowflakes. It has a thick white stripe across the top where Grandma Anne embroidered *Bernadette* in perfectly beautiful letters. Victor's is dark, dark green with St. Nicholas and a huge sack of toys. His name goes across the top of his, too. One time, though, Mama caught us and said we're not allowed to do that. Grandma put a lot of hard work and love into those stockings and she was not about to have them left on the floor and eaten by the dog. I wouldn't have left them floor for the dog. But we didn't do it again after that.

"For real, Victor!" I answered his question. "Right, Mama?"

"Right you are, Bernadette. But Advent is a long time. It's best not to be too excited about Christmas yet. We need to focus on Advent while it's here. What did Miss D say about

Advent?"

Miss D is my teacher this year. She's pretty good at explaining things. When she uses a big word, she always asks if we understand what it means. She likes to tell us how it's important to learn new words and new ideas in first grade.

"Oh, Miss D didn't say too much about Advent," I answered. "She just said about candles and stuff. Then we worked on learning an Advent song. 'Come on, Come on, You Mean Well,' it's called."

Mama bunched up her mouth in a puzzled way and looked over at me from her spot behind the steering wheel. Matthew screamed and threw his stuffed ducky at me.

"NO, Matthew! Don't throw in the car," Mama said to the duck thrower. She turned back to me, "Bernadette, don't give Spotted Ducky back to Matthew. He'll just throw it again. Come on, Come on, You Mean Well?" she asked, definitely puzzled.

"Yes," I replied. "You know it. We're always singing it at church before Christmas. I just never knew the words before. Like this." I started singing, "Come on, come on, you mea-ea-ean well..."

"Oh! You mean 'O come, O come, Emmanuel!'"

"Well, I guess it does start with O. You're right about that," I agreed.

On Sunday, Daddy explained more about Advent before dinner. Mama lit a single candle on a wreath while he was talking. She left three candles standing there, unlit and cold.

"Mama! Light the rest of the candles!" Victor demanded.

"Victor, you know how to ask nicely," Mama corrected him.

"Mama, would you PLEASE light the rest of the candles." Victor answered.

Mama smiled. "No," she said. "Each Sunday before Christmas, we'll light one more candle. So next week, we'll have two candles burning. When all four candles are lit, then it's almost Christmas!"

I smiled about the excitement of "almost Christmas!" Victor was just worried about the candles. "Then I get to blow it out!" he demanded.

"Victor, you know how to –"

"Mama, may I PLEASE blow it out," he interrupted Mama to ask nicely.

"Yes, you may. But Bernadette gets to blow it out tomorrow," Mama answered.

"Enough about the candles!" Daddy exclaimed. "We need more than candles for Advent. We need songs! So, let's sing an Advent song. 'O Come, O come, Emmanuel,' is my favorite. Emmanuel is another name for Jesus, so that song asks Jesus to come. When will He come?"

"Christmas!" Victor and I shouted together.

Mama and Daddy started singing, "O come, O come, Emmanuel."

"Hey!" I said. "We're learning that one at school, too!"

Daddy and Mama sang it the whole way through. Then Victor and I tried to join in. I knew most of the words. Victor got some of them. Matthew actually tried to sing, too. He doesn't really know too many words because he's only one year old. He likes to say "O-o-o-o-o-o-o" in a kind of singing voice when everybody else is singing. He's pretty funny when he does it.

"That's pretty good!" Daddy said. "Let's try it in Latin now!"

"Let's eat dinner now," Mama suggested. "I'm tired and hungry." She smiled a thin smile at Daddy and began dishing out the chicken casserole onto everyone's plates. "Maybe you can try it in Latin after we eat?"

Mama's getting ready to have another baby. I think that baby is taking up a lot of her food, because she's hungry a lot.

"No carrots for – PLEASE no carrots for

me," Victor said as Mama dished up his dinner. She looked at him and scraped two pieces of carrot off his plate and back into the casserole. He still had four pieces of carrot on his plate. He made a grumpy face, but he didn't complain. He just scooted them way over to the edge with his fork.

"Mama, do you know if that baby is a boy or a girl?" I asked.

"No, Bernadette, I don't. Sometimes the doctors can find out, but we'll just wait until it's born to see."

"That is difficult," I said. "Because how will I know what to give it for Christmas if I don't know if it's a boy or a girl? I would like it to be a sister. Because I could really use a sister," I made a face at Matthew, who had figured out how to spill out his sippy cup. He was happily pouring milk into his casserole and mushing it up. I watched him smear a handful of milky casserole noodles into his hair.

"I mean, look at Matthew! Yuck-o! A baby

sister wouldn't do that. Also, if it's a baby sister, she'll want a more interesting present. Like something involving a shiny ribbon or a sparkly jewel. Victor and Matthew, well I don't know what to give them." I looked at Matthew's mess again. "Maybe something involving dirt?"

"Oh, I don't know, Bernadette," Mama said after she finished chewing the bite that was already in her mouth. "I think you were pretty messy before you were two!" She glanced at Matthew again. "Well, maybe not quite as messy as Matthew!"

He squealed in delight at the attention and lobbed a handful of noodles at the dog. That didn't go well with Daddy. After the dog and noodle event was handled, Mama continued. "I think either a tiny boy or a tiny girl will be just delightful. The new baby will be so tiny on Christmas, that you don't need to get a present for him or her."